Lola

AND THE GIANT ARMOUR

MILLIE GREEN

Dedication

To my Mum, Dad and brother.

And of course, my little cousin Lola

x

Introduction

Once there lived a girl called Lola.

Now Lola may sound brave, but she was very shy and if you would like to know if Lola can overcome that, then read on...

Meet The Characters

Lola

A brave knight and the hero of the story.

Princess Millie

A fantastic chess player.

Prince Oliver

A funny joker.

King Matt

A great king

Queen Laura

A fabulous Queen.

Oscar the Dragon

The mythical beast

The Wise Old Grandparents

Wise and old.

Servant Paul

A clumsy servant.

Servant Amy

A kind and useful servant

Chapter 1

LOLA'S FEAR

Lola's Fear

Lola was just an ordinary girl living an ordinary life. But Lola had a secret. She was shy. Now Lola had done things you needed to be brave for, but Lola wasn't shy about that kind of thing. She was scared of asking for help. And because of that, Lola always got something wrong in every lesson at school - because she never asked for help. She was always guessing at questions.

Now the problem was that Lola didn't like asking her friends for help, either. But one day, Lola was reading a book and in the pages of the book about enchanted armour, she found a page on the magic armour which was used to fight the creature who guarded it. "But what is the creature?", thought Lola.

Then she spotted a book on the Wise Old Grandparents. She made up her mind. She was going to find the Wise Old Grandparents! She took the book with her to find them.

Then she remembered that she didn't like asking for help. She was thinking so hard that she walked into a tree!

"Ouch!", she said. But still she thought it was time to overcome her fear.

After pulling out a few splinters, revealing cuts underneath, she set off again until she reached the castle-like thing. It looked more like a turret than anything. She looked at the book. It was the same turret as in the book. She had found the Wise Old Grandparents! She knocked, and entered.

Chapter 2

THE WISE OLD GRANDPARENTS

The Wise Old Grandparents

The Wise Old Grandparents were sat at a scrubbed wooden table, drinking tea and reading the newspaper. They looked up as Lola entered.

"What do you want?", said the Wise Old Grandad. "Colin! Look!", said the Wise Old Grandma. "She's been travelling. I can tell. Look, she has cuts everywhere. Let her in and see what she has to say."

She let Lola in and with a wave of her hand, the cuts healed.

"Thanks!", said Lola. She sat down. "I need help", Lola told them. "I need to find the magic armour". "Okaaaay", said the Wise Old Grandma slowly. "It's in Queen Laura and King Matt's castle." "Thanks!", Lola said again. She turned to go. "Wait", said Lola, "where's that?".

The Wise Old Grandma said, "It's 100 miles north. Just keep going."

"Thanks!", Lola said again.

She turned to go. "Wait!", said the Wise Old Grandma. "You need sleep before you set off again."

"I agree Beth", said the Wise Old Grandad "sleep in our spare bed."

"Thanks", said Lola for a fourth time. Saying thanks was something you had to do a lot when you met kind people!

She went to bed. When she awoke, she got dressed and packed up her things before going down for breakfast.

"Thanks for everything", said Lola and she left. She walked 100 miles north before she reached the castle.

She knocked and two heads poked out. It looked like the prince and princess.

"I'm Prince Oliver and this is Princess Millie", said the prince. "Come in".

Lola entered. She walked past lots of pictures as she walked along the corridor. She followed them all the way into the dining hall for breakfast.

"Chicken Nuggets, my favourite!", exclaimed Lola excitedly. She sat down in the guest's chair opposite the king and queen.

Breakfast was delicious, partly because it was chicken nuggets. Then she went to play a game in the prince and princess' room. Then lunch - fried eggs. Then they went to play football before a roast dinner and then bed.

"What a day!", thought Lola and she drifted off to sleep.

Chapter 3

THE ARMOUR AND
THE DRAGON

The Armour And The Dragon

Lola woke to screaming downstairs. She grabbed her ear defenders that the Wise Old Grandparents had given her and put them on. She got dressed and went down for breakfast to find Servant Amy clearing up a smashed plate.

"What happened?", Lola asked Millie.

"Servant Paul has smashed another plate", said Millie.

"What, has it happened before?", asked Lola, intrigued.

"Yes, that's the fifteenth plate he's smashed since I've known him", said Oliver coming over. "It happens **ALL THE TIME**", they said together.

After a delicious meal of sausages, eggs and bacon Lola went back up to her room and packed up. She passed servant Paul, who said goodbye to a plant instead of Lola. Oliver and Millie rolled their eyes at her, but Lola said, "Bye Paul, thanks for everything."

"Thanks, Laura", said Paul, clumsily.

"I might come back, I don't know", added Lola.

"Okay, Matt", said Paul.

Lola said goodbye to everybody including Queen Laura and King Matt who came in to see Lola off. "Bye!", Lola called as the doors closed.

Lola set off with the map that Millie and Oliver had given her. After walking 20 miles, she came to the armoury. And inside was the magic armour. She had done it!

She grabbed the armour. It was massive, but when she grabbed it, it shrank to fit her, and it produced a snowy white horse! It had a golden seat with an identical golden mask. It had a whip and a sword and shield. Lola grabbed them and raced out, but as she was riding, she hit a dragon.

She looked at the map and the map read

Oscar the Dragon's Cave - Keeper of the Magic Armour

"Ut-oh", said Lola - she had met the creature.

Oscar opened his gleaming red eyes and stood up. He glared down at Lola. He opened his mouth and set fire to a nearby tree. Lola turned her horse to face the tree. She slapped its leg with her whip, and it opened its mouth. It blew snow at the tree. The tree stopped smoking.

"Wow," said Lola. "I'm going to call you Snowy".

Oscar blew fire, but Lola was ready. She told Snowy to do what she could do. She reared and water flew out of her hooves and froze in midair. It fell on the dragon's foot, and by the look of it, it had injured it. Lola said, "I didn't mean to hurt you. Let me help you."

The dragon sat down and held out it's scaly blue leg and Lola bandaged it up for him. Oscar roared in a way to say thank you.

Then he took off.

He breathed fire again and the flames twisted into....

"Thank you. I will never harm you again. I'm never coming back. I'm going to live with my Mum. Bye."

And he flew into the sunset.

"Bye Oscar", said Lola, waving.

Chapter 4

L.M.O

FRIENDS FOREVER

L.M.O Friends Forever

Lola rode back to Queen Laura and King Matt's castle. She tied snowy securely to the apple tree and walked inside. Millie and Oliver were playing chess in the corridor.

"Lola!", they both yelled.

"Hi", said Lola.

"You survived!", said Oliver.

"Why aren't you in the kitchen or your bedroom?", asked Lola.

"We're having a triple bed put in our room in case you wanted to stay", said Millie.

"And servant Paul has smashed his fourth frying pan", said Oliver suddenly looking quite wary for a second before looking amazed at Lola surviving again.

"No one has ever survived before", said Millie looking equally amazed.

"Yes, I survived", said Lola "by helping the dragon."

"You helped it?", said Oliver in disbelief.

"Yes, because I injured it. Snowy…"

"Who is Snowy?", interrupted Oliver.

"My horse", said Lola.

"You have a horse?", said Millie "can we see it?"

"Yes. After I have finished my sentence! Right, as I was saying, Snowy blew water at a jet of flames and they froze and landed on the dragon's foot. I bandaged it up, and it flew away." "Wow! Now let's see that horse!", said Oliver.

Lola led them out into the garden. Snowy was eating an apple that had fallen off the tree.

"It's beautiful!", said Millie.

"You can pat her if you like", said Lola.

The royal children rushed forwards and patted snowy.

"Come on", said Lola. "Let's take a ride. Oh, and by the way, I would love to stay with you, thank you." She slapped Snowy's leg and they were off around the castle.

"This is fun", said Oliver and Millie happily.

Lola rode once around the castle, then went back to the apple tree and tied snowy to the trunk and picked an apple. They went back into the corridor and Millie and Oliver finished the chess game. Millie, who was the white pieces, won but it was very close. It was king versus king, but Oliver made a stupid move and Millie got him. An hour later there was a "Not again!" from the kitchen. Oliver poked his head around the door.

"Servant Paul has dented cutlery again", said Oliver, reappearing.

"He has dented twenty pieces of cutlery now", said Millie.

They went up to bed. Lola on top of the new triple bunkbed, then Millie, then Oliver.

"Good night" came Millie's voice.

"Night", said Lola and she drifted off to sleep.

Lola woke on the 23rd of July very excited as it was her birthday. She got a new grooming brush from Oliver and Millie, a dustpan and brush from Servant Paul, new plates and cutlery from Servant Amy and a crown from her new parents – the King and Queen. She had a wonderful day.

The next day, Oliver and Millie told her that Queen Laura was having triplets in September Lola was excited. She Oliver and Millie had thought of three names Harry, James and Scarlet. The babies came on September the 13th. They were very cute. The babies were given seats, which meant they could safely ride Snowy. They loved it.

Two Years Later...

Two years later, Oliver, Millie and Lola were all teenagers, and the toddlers were getting on well - they were walking and talking at least! A few days later, Lola received two letters. One congratulating her on surviving in her quest for the armour, and the other was from Oscar's dragon keeper. It read:

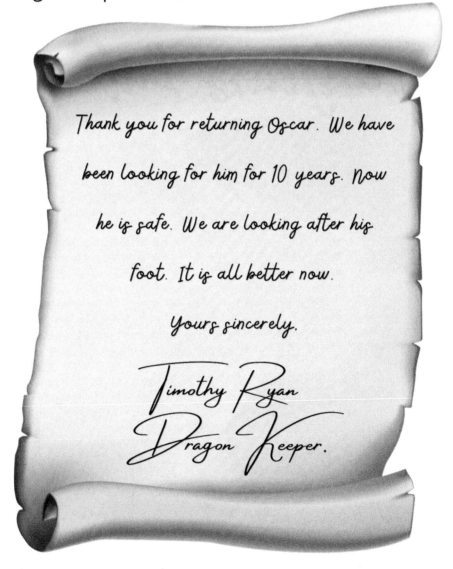

Thank you for returning Oscar. We have been looking for him for 10 years. Now he is safe. We are looking after his foot. It is all better now.

Yours sincerely,

Timothy Ryan
Dragon Keeper.

Lola was enjoying her new home very much. She was good at chess and good at helping the little children. One day Lola was bored. She went to see Snowy and noticed that she had some company! It would appear that Snowy's brothers and sisters had all come to join her! There were three more white horses and two brown. She called the other children to her.

"I have horses for each of you - girls, you can have the white and boys brown."

They each chose a horse and they were off, following Lola's lead.

Chapter 5

ABOVE
AND BEYOND

Above and Beyond

Lola had settled into life in the castle and the children were all improving at horse riding. She received a message from the mayor announcing that a party would be held at the castle in honour of Lola and her bravery! Everyone she knew would be coming.

Lola asked Servant Amy to open up the castle doors (Servant Paul had fallen down the stairs the last time he opened the doors!).

The feast was wonderful! The Wise Old Grandma and Grandad came. Lola was presented with a certificate by the mayor to congratulate her for surviving, and another one from the Wise Old Grandparents congratulating her on overcoming her fear.

Lola and her new family were happy and getting on well with their riding. However, Lola's quest to find the armour had given her a sense of adventure.

"I think it's time for an adventure", said Lola.
"I think so too", said Millie "but first you need to solve my riddle!"
"Okay", said Lola "let's hear it".

"What appears once in a minute, twice in a moment, but not once in a thousand years?", asked Millie.

"Once in a minute… twice in a moment… The letter M!" shouted Lola.

Millie nodded.

"Yes!" said Lola.

"You're good at riddles", said Oliver.

"I know", said Lola "because a few years ago, I learnt to ask for help. Right, let's get on with the adventure!"

They went outside and slapped the legs of their horses. With Lola wearing her armour, they disappeared into the sunset.

The End

.

Printed in Great Britain
by Amazon